Grandmother's Hope Chest:
The Running Rooster

By Rebekah Wilson

Hope Chest Legacy, INC.
2003

Hope Chest Legacy, INC.
PO Box 1398
Littlerock, CA. 93543
(888) 554-7292
www.HopeChestLegacy.com

ISBN# 1-59565-002-4

Printed in the United States of America
First Edition - June 2004

Dedicated to my mother,

Gladys Lucille Keen,
(1935-1983)

who placed the first needle in my hand,
taught me my first stitch,
and left me with a lifelong love of sewing...

About the Author...

Rebekah Wilson is the author of *The Hope Chest: A Legacy of Love* which has been blessing families worldwide. Together with her husband Edward, they are working to create a deeper understanding of what the hope chest truly is; and to help instill the traditional value and legacy of the hope chest for today's families and future generations.

Rebekah has enjoyed sewing by hand since a very young age. She worked as a nurse for several years until she met her husband, an LAPD police officer. With the birth of their first child, Rebekah became a stay-at-home mother. The Wilson family homeschools, lives in the country and enjoys time together.

Rebekah and her husband Edward have seven children (three girls and four boys). Rebekah enjoys writing and gives full credit to God alone for her inspiration.

If you would like to contact Rebekah, please visit her website at:

www.HopeChestLegacy.com

Forward...

Grandmother's Hope Chest is a series of twelve books designed to entertain a young girl and teach her to sew by hand. As Grandmother and Lucie go through the hope chest together, the items they come across become special projects for Lucie to recreate. Following the story of Lucie and her Grandmother, the reader and listener will learn simple basic stitches and complete easy, useful, practical projects to use today or place in the child's hope chest for her future home.

Throughout the series, Grandmother reveals a legacy for Lucie through family memories, traditions, history and heirlooms that have been stored in the hope chest. Through Grandmother, we learn how ordinary items become special treasures due to the memories they hold and the people they reflect. This is a lost part of the hope chest, and one the author hopes to revive for the next generation of children.

The books in this series are written with young children in mind, and for mothers who have never learned to sew by hand. The author has taken the liberty to write directions and use items that will make learning easier for new beginners. For instance, directions have been simplified with only very basic information so as not to overwhelm the learner. In place of straight pins, safety pins may be used to keep little fingers and hands from being pricked. Instead of regular thread that tangles easily, quilting thread can be used.

The ultimate goal of this book is to help young girls and their mothers take their "first stitches" together, to create a lifelong joy in hand sewing, and to show through example how special and unique a hope chest can be.

Table of Contents

"Lucinda Grace!" Momma called from the guest bedroom, "Come and help me make Grandmother's bed."

Lucinda, otherwise known as "Lucie", gave one more very long glance up and down the street before she sighed and turned away from the large front windows to go help Momma. Waiting was SO hard sometimes...

Lucie carefully helped Momma place the new, clean sheets on Grandmother's bed and fluff the pillows. She was smoothing the top quilt to get the last wrinkles out when she heard her brother Thomas call "They're here! They're here!" Without a backward glance Lucie ran through the doorway, out through the front door and nearly ran into Thomas who had stopped next to the driveway while Daddy helped Grandmother from the car.

Thomas and Lucie stood side by side, shyly taking glances at the passenger side of the car to get a glimpse of Grandmother. Grandmother was Momma's momma and had always lived faraway in Florida. But now, Grandmother was going to live with Lucie and her family.

Lucie was very excited, but a little scared too. She was only two years old when Grandmother had come to visit before. That was five years ago. Lucie could not remember Grandmother at all!

As Daddy moved aside to allow Grandmother to walk towards the house, Lucie was able to see her for the first time. Grandmother's smile was the happiest one Lucie could ever remember seeing and Lucie couldn't help but smile back.

Grandmother's eyes crinkled at the corners as she smiled and looked at Lucie, and Lucie simply stood still, gazing back. Grandmother had lots of gray hair. It was parted down the middle, pulled back and wrapped into a bun at the top of her head. She had a pair of glasses that were silver and shiny and sparkled in the sunshine.

Grandmother looked at Thomas and reached out to cup his chin in her soft hand. "You've grown so much I can hardly recognize you!" she said. "You look just like your Daddy!"

Thomas grinned, then looked down at his feet shyly, trying to hide his face which had turned a shade redder than it had been before.

"And Lucie! You have HAIR!" Grandmother said laughing softly. "The last time I saw you, you were as bald as that little baby your Momma is holding. Why, look at those long, thick braids," Grandmother said, as she reached out and fingered Lucie's twin braids, then gently brushed Lucie's cheek with her cool soft fingers.

Lucie could smell roses on Grandmother's hands. Lucie liked roses. Lucie liked her Grandmother too.

Momma called from the porch for Grandmother to come in and sit down and rest. Lemonade and oatmeal cookies were waiting for her. Lucie knew Momma had made the cookies special just for Grandmother. She had watched Momma earlier in the morning as the cookies were put into the oven. Momma always put cinnamon in the oatmeal cookies because she said it made them taste extra special that way. Lucie was allowed to taste the first cookie that was cool enough, to make sure they were okay. Momma's cookies were always okay, but

Momma would let Thomas and Lucie test each batch just to make sure.

Lucie followed Grandmother into the house and stood near the window as Grandmother fussed over baby Anna. Anna cried at the strange face in front of her until Grandmother started singing softly to her...

This is my Father's world,
And to my listening ears
All nature sings, and round me rings
The music of the spheres.
This is my Father's world:
I rest me in the thought
Of rocks and trees, of skies and seas—
His hand the wonders wrought.

This is my Father's world,
The birds their carols raise,
The morning light, the lily white,
Declare their Maker's praise.
This is my Father's world:
He shines in all that's fair;
In the rustling grass I hear Him pass,
He speaks to me everywhere.

This is my Father's world,
O let me ne'er forget
That though the wrong seems oft so strong,
God is the Ruler yet.
This is my Father's world:
The battle is not done;
Jesus who died shall be satisfied,
And earth and heav'n be one.

Momma chuckled as she saw Lucie's face. "Where do you think I learned that hymn Lucie? Your Grandmother sang that to me when I was a baby, and I sang it to Thomas, and you, and now Anna."

"There's many more where that hymn came from. There's nothing better than a good hymn and a rocking chair to put a fussy baby to sleep," Grandmother said as she settled into the soft oversized, brown sofa and gave a long deep sigh of pleasure. "Oh this does feel nice!" she said with a smile and baby Anna gurgled at her.

Lucie sat quietly and listened as Momma and Grandmother talked. Daddy was coming and going, bringing in Grandmother's belongings and placing them in her new room. Lucie didn't notice what her father was bringing in until she suddenly saw Mr. Edwards, their neighbor, coming through the doorway backwards.

Lucie was all eyes as Mr. Edwards and her father struggled to bring in a large wooden box. It barely fit through the doorway and looked very old and very heavy.

The two men disappeared into the hallway and Lucie leaned over as far as she could to watch it go through Grandmother's bedroom doorway.

"I'm so glad you brought it! I wasn't sure if you would or not." Momma said.

"Oh of course I brought it. That will be Lucie's one day." Grandmother said and watched Lucie's eyes widen in surprise.

"What is it Grandmother?" Lucie asked, almost in a whisper.

"Why, it's a hope chest. Your Momma has one that her daddy made for her, that one is mine. When you're older it will be yours." Grandmother explained.

"Mine? What will I do with it?" Lucie asked.

That made Grandmother smile. "What will you do with it? That's a big question," she said, rocking back and forth, thinking for several moments.

"Well, it will help you learn many things you need to know. One day, when you're older and get married, it will be a wonderful blessing for you."

"Oh," said Lucie, not sure what Grandmother was talking about. "Do I have to wait that long? Can't I learn now?"

Lucie was still looking down the hallway and did not see her Momma's wink and her Grandmother's answering nod...

Several days later, Lucie walked slowly past Grandmother's open door. She knew Grandmother was sitting in her rocking chair reading and did not want to disturb her. Lucie just wanted to peek once more at the wooden box Grandmother called a hope chest. It was *so* big! And it was shiny and smooth. There were a few scratches she could see as the light from the window fell on it. But it was beautiful. Daddy had told her it was made of maple wood from the same trees that maple syrup comes from. Lucie wondered if it smelled like maple syrup too…

"Lucie? Is that you peeking around my doorway?" Grandmother asked.

Lucie moved forward a little, still somewhat shy of her Grandmother. "Yes, I was just looking at the hope chest again. It's very shiny."

"Yes it is. Come sit down here next to me and I'll tell you a little about this chest," Grandmother said, moving things aside on her bed to make room for Lucie.

"This chest was built by my grandfather for my mother when she was young. That was your great-grandmother. It's pretty old isn't it?" Grandmother asked.

Lucie nodded quietly.

"The wood came from maple trees on the farm where my mother grew up. Each winter they would tap the trees and gather the maple sap to boil down for maple sugar. Those trees would help keep the farm going because my great-grandfather would sell the maple syrup for cash money. Of course they kept plenty of syrup for themselves too! My mother and her brothers would pour the syrup over fresh snow and eat it for a treat. They would make candy with it too. Mother said when it was maple sugaring time, you could smell it in the wind because all the neighbors would be boiling the sap too," said Grandmother.

"Wow!" Lucie said in wonder. "Does the hope chest smell like maple syrup too?"

Grandmother laughed. "I don't think so. If it did it doesn't anymore."

"Oh," said Lucie, a little disappointed.

"Would you like to see inside Lucie?" Grandmother asked.

"Oh YES!" Lucie said, hardly breathing.

Grandmother went over to her dresser and opened the top drawer. She reached in and pulled something long and slender out and held it up for Lucie to see.

"A key!" Lucie said in surprise.

Grandmother bent over and placed the key in the lock. As the key turned there was a slight scrapping sound and then it stopped. Grandmother pulled the key out, placed it in her pocket, then lifted the lid.

Lucie wasn't sure what she expected to see. She leaned forward eagerly, as so many wonderful things appeared before her eyes.

There were stacks of papers and old photographs. A patchwork quilt had been carefully folded and put on one side. Lucie could see baby clothes and a baby bonnet. A stack of envelopes were tied together with a thin pink ribbon. A small wood picture frame held a curled lock of dark hair under the glass. There were old military medals in a corner of the top tray. Next to the army medals sat a pearl necklace and some silver chains and pieces of old jewelry. A floppy cloth doll smiled back at Lucie from the top of her little perch of scrapbooks.

"Each item in this chest is very special to me," Grandmother said quietly. She picked up the cloth doll and smiled, "This was my 'best doll' when I was a little girl." Grandmother said as she adjusted the doll's dress before putting her back in place on top of the scrapbooks.

"This stack of letters were from your grandfather when we were courting. I saved every single one," said Grandmother and moved them aside.

"This lock of hair was from my grandmother. She gave it to my grandfather in 1917 when he was sent to France during World War I. Grandfather made this little wooden frame to put the hair in so it wouldn't get lost. He carved the designs on it with his pocketknife while he was gone. When the war was over and he came home, he gave this back to my grandmother and then he got down on his knees and asked her to marry him." Grandmother smiled at the thought. She took the frame and held it up next to Lucie's head.

"Yes, I thought so!" Grandmother said. "You have the same color hair she did."

That made Lucie smile. She liked that.

"Maybe when your Momma trims your hair, we can take a little snip and put it in this frame for you, right next to your great-great-grandmother's curl. Then you can show your own little girl one day," Grandmother said. She carefully put the frame back and moved a few more things around.

Lucie and Grandmother spent a long time going through the chest. Grandmother would explain about each item, then carefully replace it in the chest. Lucie was enjoying herself very much and did not want this time to end. Beneath every item was something more interesting and more wonderful than Lucie had already seen. Everything in the chest was special to Grandmother and now they were becoming special to Lucie too.

Several days later Lucie once more peeked around Grandmother's doorway. She was hoping Grandmother would open the chest again.

"Lucie, come in and sit down honey," came Grandmother's voice.

Lucie walked into the room and found Grandmother sewing a pillowcase. Bright red thread went in and out of the fabric and Lucie could see a pretty red bow being formed.

"That's very pretty," said Lucie. "What are you making?"

"A pillowcase for your hope chest, Lucie. I'll make two so they match," Grandmother said.

"Oh…thank you," said Lucie. She stood next to Grandmother's rocking chair and watched her for several minutes. At first it was hard to figure out what Grandmother was doing. As Lucie watched, she noticed that Grandmother's needle and the thread were following the lines on top of the pillowcase. It didn't look too hard; in fact it looked easy and Lucie wanted to try.

"Is it hard to sew, Grandmother?" Lucie asked timidly.

"No, not really. The more you sew the easier it gets," was Grandmother's reply.

"Do you think I could try?" Lucie asked.

"Well now...I was hoping you would say that," Grandmother said with a gentle smile. "I have some extra needles and thread you can use. You need to start at the beginning and learn your stitches before you can do this fancy sewing. Do you still want to try?"

"Oh YES!" Lucie said, and almost jumped up in her excitement.

"Let me show you something..." Grandmother said. She opened the hope chest and took out a small bundle, placing it in her lap.

"This was your Momma's very first sewing project," said Grandmother. She lifted up a cream colored potholder that had a running rooster stitched in red thread. "She gave this to me a long time ago and it has always been my favorite potholder," Grandmother explained.

"Momma made that?" Lucie said, "How old was she?"

"Oh, about your age. I think she was almost seven years old," Grandmother replied.

"You can make one too Lucie. This is a very simple stitch to learn. That's how you learn to sew, one stitch at a time." she said and handed the potholder to Lucie.

Lucie traced the rooster with her finger. It was just a little bumpy where the stitches went in and out of the fabric.

"This is a silly rooster," said Lucie. "It looks like it's running to catch something."

Grandmother chuckled. "A very silly rooster! It must be after a fly! Now Lucie, this potholder will teach you the *Running Stitch* and the *Overcasting Stitch* and they are both simple stitches you will use all the time in sewing. Should we start?" Grandmother asked.

Lucie nodded eagerly and scooted closer to Grandmother so she could see better.

The Running Rooster Potholder:

Items needed: 10 ½" x 9" printed fabric for backing, 100% cotton batting cut in two pieces each measuring 8½" x 7", one piece of white muslin measuring 8½" x 7" for the top, 1 skein DMC embroidery floss #304 (deep red), 1 skein of embroidery floss to match the backing fabric, 1 embroidery needle size #9, 1 spool of white quilting thread, 1 pair of small trimming scissors (3-4" in length), 1 packet of medium sized safety pins or straight pins (the choice is yours.)

Preparation: Pre-wash your fabrics before cutting, iron flat. There are three layers to this potholder. The back of the potholder is called the "backing", the inner cushioned area is called the "batting" and the white muslin is the "top" of the potholder. Using the "Running Rooster" pattern in the back of this book, place your white muslin block over the pattern and center the rooster on the block. Trace the pattern lines with a pencil.

Place the pretty side of your backing fabric face DOWN on a tabletop. Center the two cotton batting pieces over the backing fabric. Place your white muslin over the batting with all edges meeting and even. Make sure your rooster pattern lines are looking up at you.

Basic Instructions: (in-depth details given throughout the story text)

- ♥ Baste around the top edge of potholder.
- ♥ Outline the "Running Rooster" in red embroidery floss using the Running Stitch.
- ♥ Fold printed edges over and pin in place.
- ♥ Sew edges in place using Overcast Stitch.
- ♥ Take out Basting Stitches.
- ♥ Finished!

Grandmother handed Lucie the fabrics and batting and watched as she put them together in layers.

"Now what do I do?" asked Lucie.

"First we thread our needle with the quilting thread. Do you know how to thread a needle?" Grandmother asked.

"No. I've watched Momma do it, but I never tried before," Lucie said.

"Let me show you how," said Grandmother. "First we trim the end of the thread flat with a pair of scissors. This prevents any frayed ends from splitting or bending and causing trouble going through the eye of the needle."

To thread your needle—carefully hold the tip of the thread in your left hand between your finger and thumb. With your right hand, hold your needle along the shaft so the "eye" or hole of your needle is up and ready for the thread to be put through. Slowly open your finger and thumb holding the thread until you can "just barely" see the tip of the thread. Place the eye of your needle over the thread tip and gently wiggle the needle back and forth as you push down. This will allow the thread to "slide through the eye" of your needle. If your thread tip begins to split, you may need to moisten the tip by placing it in your mouth for a spilt second—this binds the ends together for easier threading. Once the thread is poking through the eye, squeeze your thumb and finger together to hold the needle in place, and with your right hand take the thread and pull through a little more. Your needle is now threaded. Be careful not to pull on your thread too much while sewing and pull the thread off of your needle! (When your needle is threaded, you will have one long piece of thread going through the eye of your needle. The thread will be bent in half and folded where the needle's eye is. (See illustration pg 30.) You will have a long and short part to your thread. The longer end of your thread will have your knot at the end of it; the shorter end of your thread will stay as is. When you begin sewing and using up your longer piece of thread and it becomes shorter, simply pull a little of your shorter piece through the eye to "lengthen" the long one. Make sure while sewing to _always_ leave enough thread to make a knot and end your sewing!)

"Oh I see! That's not hard at all," said Lucie. "I don't put the thread through the needle, I put the needle on the thread!"

"Yes, it's very easy. Do you know how to make a knot at the end of the thread?" Grandmother asked.

"No, is that hard?" Lucie asked.

"Certainly not...maybe a little tricky at first, but it is very easy when you learn how," Grandmother said.

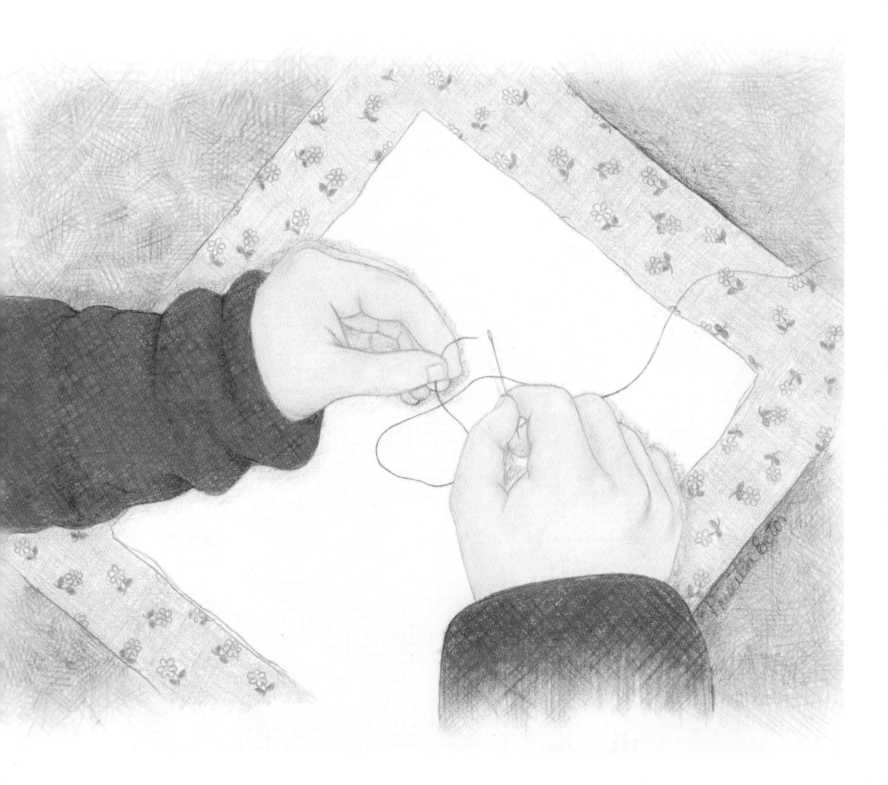

To knot your thread—wrap the end of your thread around the tip of your left finger. Place your thumb on top of the thread and "roll" the thread off of your finger. This will cause the thread to twist around itself inside the loop on your finger. With your middle finger, press your fingernail onto the thread JUST above the twisted loop and then slide the thread between your fingernail and your thumb until the twisted loop has pulled itself into a small, tiny knot at the end of your thread.

"Very good Lucie!" Grandmother said. "You learned that very well."

"Now what do I do?" Lucie asked.

"Now we start basting around the edge of your white muslin."

"Why?" Lucie asked, shocked. "That's what Momma does with the turkey at Thanksgiving!" Lucie couldn't understand what basting had to do with sewing.

Grandmother laughed for a long time before she could talk again. "No, there are two special stitches called *Even Basting Stitch* and *Uneven Basting Stitch*," Grandmother explained.

Basting Stitches: Basting is VERY important when you have several layers you will be sewing. Basting Stitches help to "hold" the fabric in place instead of using pins. This way, as you work on your potholder, the fabric will not slide around and bunch up making wrinkles or cause the edges to be off-balance. There are two kinds of basting stitches, the Even Basting stitch and the Uneven Basting stitch.

The *Even Basting Stitch* has the stitches evenly placed, as in the diagram below.

━ ━ ━ ━ ━ ━ ━ ━ ━ ━ ━ ━ ━ ━ ━ ━

The *Uneven Basting Stitch* has a long stitch, then a short stitch, then a long stitch and then a short stitch. This has more "holding power" as the smaller stitches between the longer ones will not move or give as easily. You may use either stitch for basting your potholder.

━ • ━ • ━ • ━ • ━ • ━ • ━ • ━ • ━ • ━ • ━

Note: The younger the child, the longer their stitches will be. This is fine. They are just starting to learn and it is more important that they learn how to make the needle go up and down than to have small stitches closely placed together. Basting will give them a head start before we start outlining the Running Rooster and they will need smaller stitches.

"Basting stitches don't stay in forever though, we take them out when we are done with our sewing, just like we would take out pins when we were finished," Grandmother explained.

"Oh!" Lucie said. "Which stitch should I use? The Even or Uneven Stitch?"

"That depends on what you are doing. For this project we can use the Even Basting Stitch," said Grandmother.

 How do I make the Even Basting stitch?" Lucie asked.

"This is very simple," Grandmother said, picking up the layers of fabric. "We want to leave 1 inch of fabric between the edge of the white muslin and our stitching. To start, push the needle up from the backing fabric to the top, then we pull the thread all the way through until it catches on the back."

"Now, push the needle down through the fabric 1/4 to 1/2 inch from where the needle and thread have come up. Pull the thread until it stops. Push the needle up again, 1/4 to 1/2 inch from where the thread went down. Keep doing this all the way down one side, then we turn the potholder and do the next side, and continue until all four sides are basted. Be careful not to pull the needle so far that the thread is pulled out of the needle. If you do this, simply re-thread the needle, but it's easier to pay attention and not let the shorter thread slide through." Grandmother explained. She gave the fabric layers back to Lucie.

Lucie worked hard and tried to make small stitches like Grandmother, but the stitches were too big.

"I can't make them as small as you did, Grandmother! Help!" said Lucie.

"You are just learning Lucie. Keep sewing. The stitches will get smaller and you will do better. Remember, you are a little girl who is just learning how to sew! If you take big stitches it's okay, just keep working on making smaller ones and in time you will," Grandmother said.

Lucie sewed while Grandmother continued on the pillowcase. Several quiet minutes went by...

"OUCH!" cried Lucie and quickly put her finger in her mouth.

"Poke yourself?" Grandmother asked.

Lucie nodded, her finger still in her mouth and a frown on her face.

"That happens. Especially when you are first learning to sew. The more you practice, the less often you will poke yourself. You could use a thimble I guess, but they always seem to get in the way when I try them..." Grandmother said.

Lucie looked at her finger carefully, pushed on it a few times, then cautiously started sewing again.

"Grandmother, I finished the basting, how do I end it?" Lucie asked.

"Take three stitches in the *same* holes and then cut the thread," replied Grandmother.

"You mean go up and down in the same holes three times?" Lucie asked.

"Yes, we don't want to leave a knot that we can't take out later. This way, we can pull the threads out without the knot being left behind making a lump."

"Oh! The knot would get stuck! I see...I don't want any lumps on my potholder," Lucie said. "Okay, I finished it. Now what's next?"

"Thread your needle with the red embroidery floss and start on the rooster!" Grandmother said. "Embroidery floss has six strands of thread that make up the floss. Sometimes we use all six strands, and other times we need to split the floss into fewer strands. The more strands we use, the thicker the stitch will be, the fewer strands we use the thinner the stitch will be. We want a nice thick stitch for the rooster!" Grandmother explained, "So we will use all six strands of the red floss."

Note: Once the basting is finished, start to outline the Running Rooster in the red embroidery floss. Pull a strand of floss out about 18-22" in length and cut. If the child is very young, you may need to use a shorter piece. Thread your needle and knot the end.

Start from the back of the potholder and bring your needle to the front along the pattern line. Pull your thread through until the knot stops it. We will need to "sink the knot" to keep it from showing. To sink the knot, lay the back side up. Place your needle slightly in front of your knot and lift up the top layer of fabric but DO NOT pull through the fabric. Tug gently—the fabric will slowly give and stretch until a small hole has formed through the weave for the knot to slip through—then pull the needle out. Your knot should now be hidden beneath the first layer and out of sight. If your knot is large, you may need to help stretch the fabric with your needle tip and tug a little harder to help the knot pop through the fabric.

We are now ready to use the Running stitch to outline the pattern line. The Running stitch is simply an up and down stitch, where the stitches and spaces between the stitches are evenly placed as in the diagram below.

■ ■ ■ ■ ■ ■ ■ ■ ■ ■ ■ ■ ■ ■ ■ ■ ■ ■ ■

We will do the entire Running Rooster outline using this stitch. It would be best to start with the back toes of the rooster, stitch up the belly, down to the front toes, then up the chest to the wattles (beneath the chin), the head and crown, then down the back to the tail feathers and down to the back toes again.

The Running Stitch: The Running stitch is the most commonly used handsewing stitch. For this stitch, we pull the needle from the back to the front and "hide the knot." Next, place the needle tip down 1/8" from where the thread has come up through the fabric. Pull the thread through until it stops. Bring the needle tip up on the pattern line, 1/8" from where the thread has gone through the fabric for the previous stitch. Continue in this way as you follow the pattern line. Try to take small stitches and avoid long ones.

Lucie started sewing along the pattern line of the rooster. She struggled several times to pull the thread through, but Grandmother didn't say anything; she just kept sewing and humming to herself.

"Grandmother, this needle won't come through. It's too hard sometimes!" Lucie said.

"There's a trick to it, but let me explain what happens first. The needle makes a hole for the thread to follow through, and the eye of the needle is the widest part. The eye will often get stuck if you have a thick strand of thread or floss that plugs up the hole the needle made. If you look carefully at your fabric, you can see thin threads going up and down, and also sideways. These threads are the *weave* of the fabric, the actual threads that make up the fabric. When you try to pull your needle through, the weave has to separate enough to allow the needle and the thread to go through. To do this, pull your needle through as far as you can before it gets stuck at the eye, then tug quickly and firmly, and do it as you pull away from the fabric. It will pop through quickly so be ready for it," Grandmother explained.

"Oh. I see," said Lucie. She pulled her needle through as far as it would go, then tugged quick and hard and the needle flew through the fabric.

"Wow! It worked!" Lucie said.

"Of course it does. Sometimes you might need to tug a few times. Now be careful not to pull your needle right off the thread. If you aren't paying attention, your shorter thread gets shorter and shorter and then slides right out of the needle," Grandmother cautioned her.

Lucie worked a little longer and then showed her Grandmother.

"Very nice Lucie!" Grandmother said, holding the potholder in her hands and running a finger over Lucie's stitches. "Very nice!"

"Thank you. What do I do now? I'm done with the rooster," said Lucie.

"You need to leave a knot so your stitches won't come undone. The easiest way to make a knot and end your sewing, is to wrap your thread around the needle tip two times…"

"Then put your needle down close to where the thread came out, and push your needle through the backing fabric and the loops on the needle…"

"Pull your needle through the loops and the fabric until the knot catches. Then you need to "hide the knot" by tugging gently, but firmly, until the knot goes through the fabric and is hidden beneath the backing," explained Grandmother. "Just like when you pulled the needle through and it was stuck at the end, you have to tug on this too and make a hole for the knot to slide beneath the fabric so it will "hide."

Lucie tried for several minutes to "hide the knot" before it pulled through the fabric.

"I did it!" she said happily.

"Very good!" Grandmother said with approval. "You are learning very quickly and doing so well. Now we need to finish the edges and you will be all done."

To Finish the Edges— fold the bottom edge of your potholder over so the rough outer edge of your fabric is now inside touching the batting. Fold your doubled edge over onto the white muslin top. Pin in place on the white muslin with pins, go through ALL layers to hold them in place.

Next, do the same for the top of your potholder and pin in place. Now do the same for your two remaining longer sides. Carefully remove any pins that may be in the way from the previous folds. When you have the two long sides pinned in place, you may need to gently tuck in the corner folds if they are sticking out slightly (see diagram pg 41). Pin well.

With your matching embroidery floss, use an Overcast Stitch to sew the edge of the backing fabric onto the white muslin. Use three strands of your floss instead of the full six. It is easier to cut your floss, then hold it out in front of you while you pull the strands apart so the floss can dangle and untangle as you slowly pull. This prevents the floss from knotting up or tangling. Make your stitches as small and close together as you can. When you come to the corner edges, sew the open areas closed along the edge of the fold (see diagram pg 41).

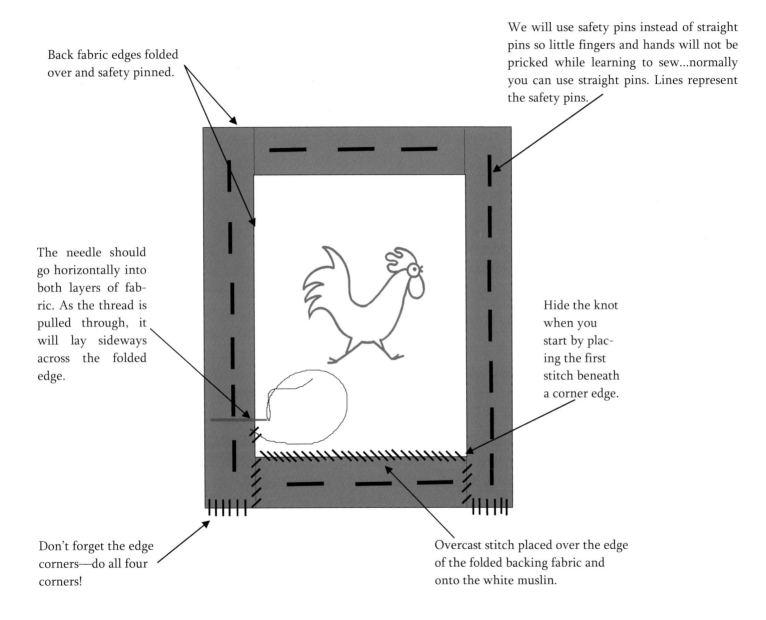

Back fabric edges folded over and safety pinned.

We will use safety pins instead of straight pins so little fingers and hands will not be pricked while learning to sew...normally you can use straight pins. Lines represent the safety pins.

The needle should go horizontally into both layers of fabric. As the thread is pulled through, it will lay sideways across the folded edge.

Hide the knot when you start by placing the first stitch beneath a corner edge.

Don't forget the edge corners—do all four corners!

Overcast stitch placed over the edge of the folded backing fabric and onto the white muslin.

"The stitch you need to use for sewing the edge of the backing to the white muslin top is called the *Overcasting Stitch*," Grandmother said.

"This stitch is simple too. Start the stitch by going under at one corner so you can push the knot under the fabric edge and hide it. Then go through the white muslin—but not into the batting! You need to sew only the white muslin and the backing edge together—not the batting. Can you do that?" Grandmother asked.

Lucie nodded slowly, "I think so."

"Good. When you go through the white muslin, just take a small straight stitch and bring the needle out through the folded fabric's edge… when you take your next stitch, the thread will lay sideways over the edge. Your needle needs to go in straight for every stitch, and the thread will lay sideways all by itself when you pull the thread through. Go all the way around the whole edge of the potholder and make sure you sew the edges at the corners too," Grandmother explained.

"Okay. This will take a long time though! Will I finish before dinner?" Lucie asked.

"I think so. It goes much faster than you think. If you don't finish, you can work on it tomorrow and finish," said Grandmother.

Lucie worked quietly for a long time. When Momma went by the doorway, she glanced in to see Lucie bent over her sewing and concentrating hard. This made Momma smile.

After a long long time, Lucie sighed and put her needle down. "I'm finished Grandmother. How do I knot the end of this?" she asked.

"You knot it just like we did for the red embroidery floss. Only be careful not to tug too hard because this thread is not as thick and will go through the fabric much easier. Tugging too hard will make the knot go through all the layers and it will be sitting on the top!" Grandmother said with a smile.

Lucie spent a few more minutes finishing up the knot, then cut the thread off even with the fabric top.

"Look Grandmother! I DID it!!!" Lucie said proudly. "Can I go show Momma?" she asked.

Grandmother nodded with a smile and watched as Lucie put the needle in the pincushion and bounced out the door...

Momma, of course, was very proud of Lucie's hard work and gave Lucie a big hug. "The hardest part of sewing is your first stitch and it gets much easier after that, doesn't it Lucie?"

"Yes it does...except when you poke yourself!" Lucie said, and showed Momma the tiny hole where the needle had pricked her finger.

Momma kissed it and gave Lucie another hug. "Want to help with dinner?" she asked.

"Yes I want to help! I made this potholder for you Momma. Can we put it with the other ones?" Lucie asked.

"Of course we can! We can use it tonight when we make dinner too...and everyone can see it!" Momma said, and placed the potholder on the top of all the other potholders. "I think this will be my favorite one from now on," Momma said proudly.

Lucie smiled...

Running Rooster Project Outline

- ♥ Pre-wash your fabric, dry and iron flat.
- ♥ Cut your printed fabric to fit 10½ x 9".
- ♥ Cut your white muslin to fit 8½ x 7".
- ♥ Cut TWO pieces of cotton batting to 8½ x 7".
- ♥ Place your white muslin top piece over the Running Rooster pattern at the back of the book. Center the pattern on your fabric. Trace the pattern with a pencil.
- ♥ Place all three layers together in order - the backing lays flat with the pretty side down, the batting is centered over the backing, and the white muslin top piece is centered over both previous layers with the traced rooster on top facing you.
- ♥ Baste around the top edge of the potholder on the white muslin, 1" from the edge.
- ♥ Use the Running Stitch to outline the Running Rooster in red embroidery floss.
- ♥ Fold the shorter sides of the printed fabric edges over once, twice, pin in place.
- ♥ Fold the long sides of the printed fabric edges over once, twice, pin in place.
- ♥ Sew all folded edges in place using the Overcast Stitch.
- ♥ Remove Basting Stitches.
- ♥ Potholder is finished! Enjoy!!!

The Running Rooster Pattern

Enjoy your finished potholder!

If you have a problem or question with this project, please contact Hope Chest Legacy at:

HopeChestLegacy@aol.com

(888) 554-7292

We will be happy to help!

About the Illustrator...

Priscilla Ector is a homeschooled student from East Tennessee, where she lives with her parents, four sisters and two brothers. Her love of drawing was evident at a very young age. She is an excellent student in all areas but especially enjoys math and literature. Other interests include painting, music and dancing with a local Christian ballet studio, where she is a company member. Being raised with "living books", she was thrilled to get the opportunity to illustrate this children's series. In the future she hopes to continue her career in illustrating children's books. She offers special thanks to her art teacher and friend, Lisa Bell, who has been invaluable for her instruction, coaching, and inspiration for this project.

CHA CHA

GROOVY

HOT DOG

DIG IT

HEP CAT

WISE GUY

A OK

PEN PAL

BOOK CLUB

WHIZ KID

LET'S READ

WRITE ME

LOVE LETTER

BE MINE

HOW NICE

TEACH ME

DREAM BOY

HOT SHOT

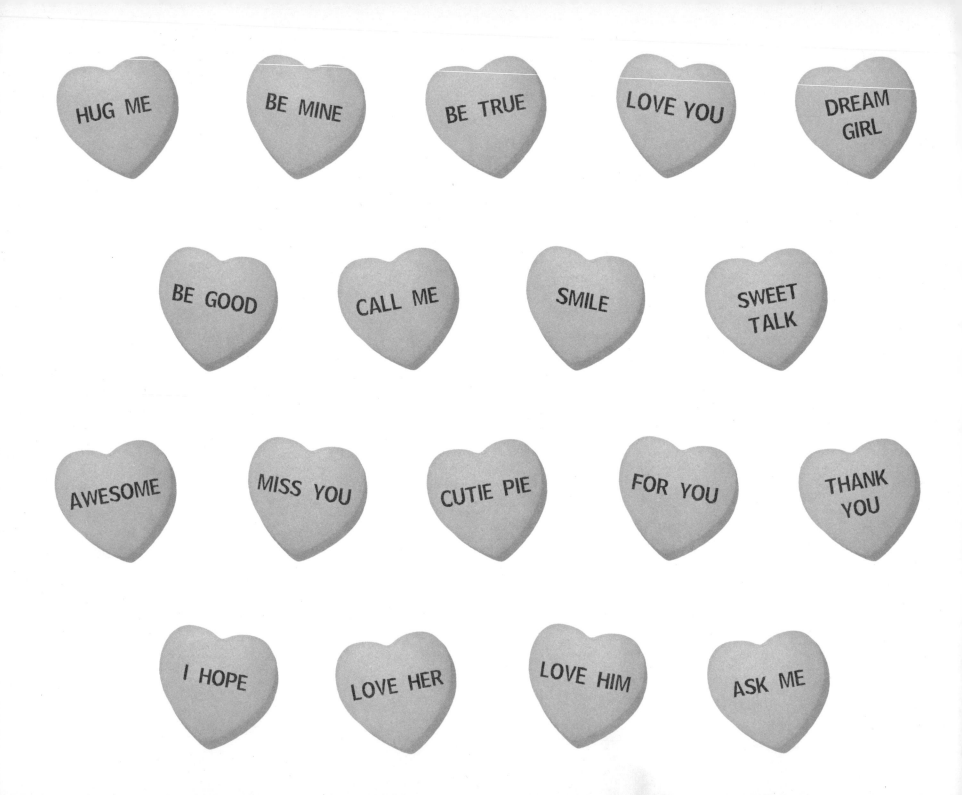

I LOVE
WORDS

Barbara Barbieri McGrath

Charlesbridge

LOVE TO: Kathleen Morse.

KISSES TO: Donna Armstrong and the staff at
Ezra Baker Elementary School in Dennis, Massachusetts.

HUGS TO: Lois MacGregor, Reading Specialist,
Hastings Elementary School in Westboro, Massachusetts.

Text copyright © 2003 by Barbara Barbieri McGrath
Illustrations copyright © 2003 by Charlesbridge Publishing
All rights reserved, including the right of reproduction in whole or in part in any form. Charlesbridge and colophon are registered
trademarks of Charlesbridge Publishing, Inc.

Published by Charlesbridge
85 Main Street
Watertown, MA 02472
(617) 926-0329
www.charlesbridge.com

Library of Congress Cataloging-in-Publication Data

McGrath, Barbara Barbieri, 1954–
  I love words / Barbara Barbieri McGrath.
    p. cm.
Summary: Introduces the letters of the alphabet and simple words,
including colors, numbers, compound words, and contractions, using Necco®
Sweethearts® candies.
  ISBN 1-57091-567-9 (reinforced for library use) — ISBN 1-57091-568-7 (softcover)
  1. Lexicology—Juvenile literature. [1. Vocabulary. 2. Alphabet. 3.
Reading readiness.] I. Title.
  P326 .M38 2003
  428.1—dc21   2002155448

Printed in South Korea

(hc) 10 9 8 7 6 5 4 3 2 1
(sc) 10 9 8 7 6 5 4 3 2 1

Display type set in Hoosker Do, designed by T-26 of Chicago, IL, USA, Segura Inc.'s Digital Type Foundry,
    started by Carlos Segura in 1994; text type set in Adobe Caslon
Printed and bound by Pacifica Comunications, South Korea
Production supervision by Brian G. Walker
Designed by Susan Mallory Sherman

Necco® and Sweethearts® are registered trademarks of the
New England Confectionery Company.

Let's learn to read words. There's no time like now.
You'll love to read once you know how.

Here are the letters *A* through Z.
Uppercase and lowercase letters to see.

Each letter has its own special sound.
To begin to make words, move them around.

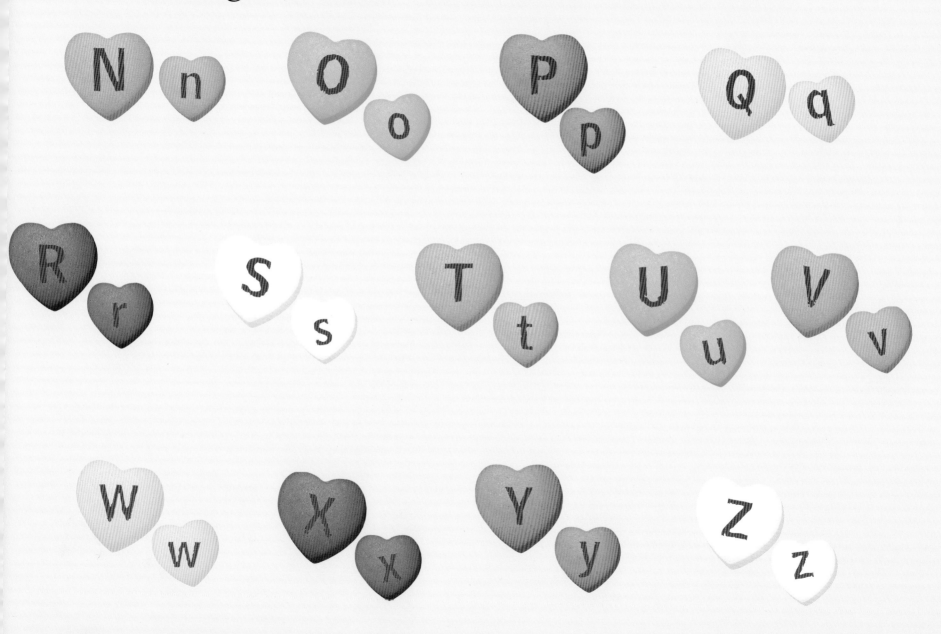

Use vowels so that the words are heard.
They're an important part of every word.

Pat, pet, pit, pot, put, oh my…
A vowel can sometimes be a Y.

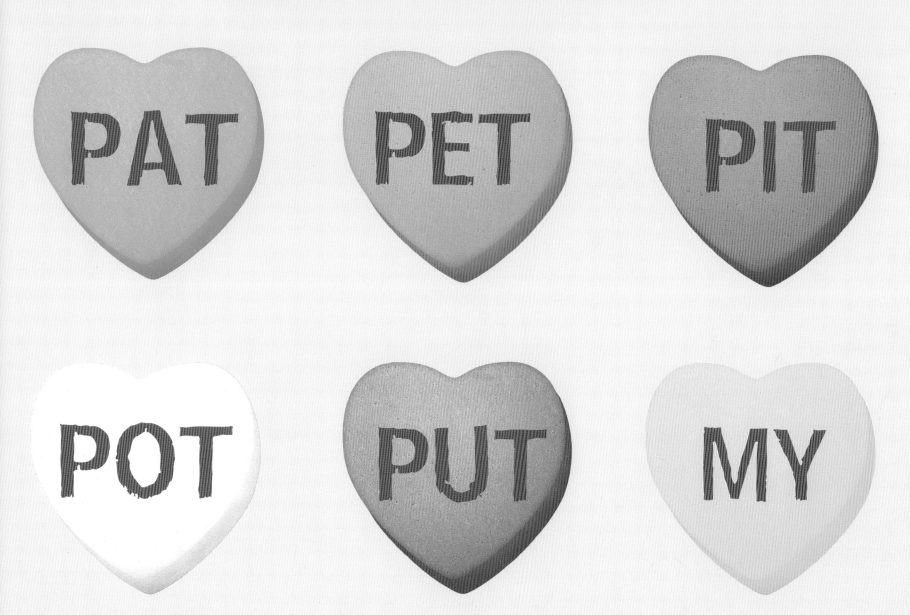

A long vowel "a" means you hear *A* in **say.**

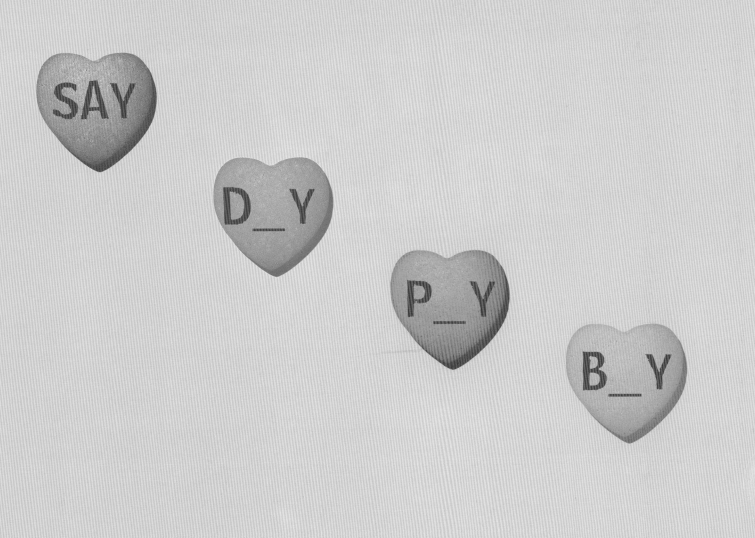

The short "a" in **can** does not sound that way.

Try words without vowels. No matter how hard you try…

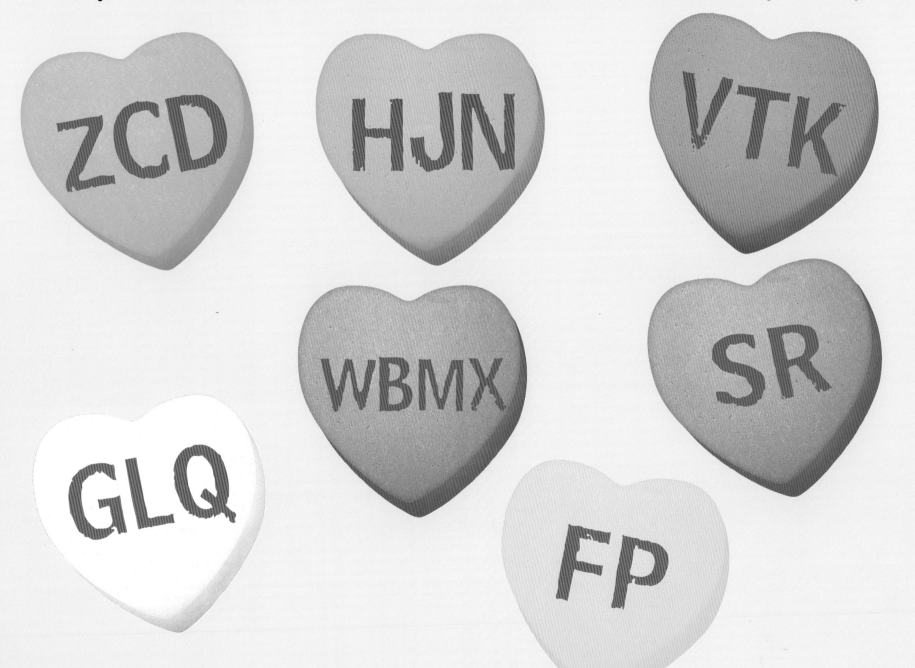

Consonants need vowels. And now you know why.

Look at these words with all your might;
Try to know them all by sight.

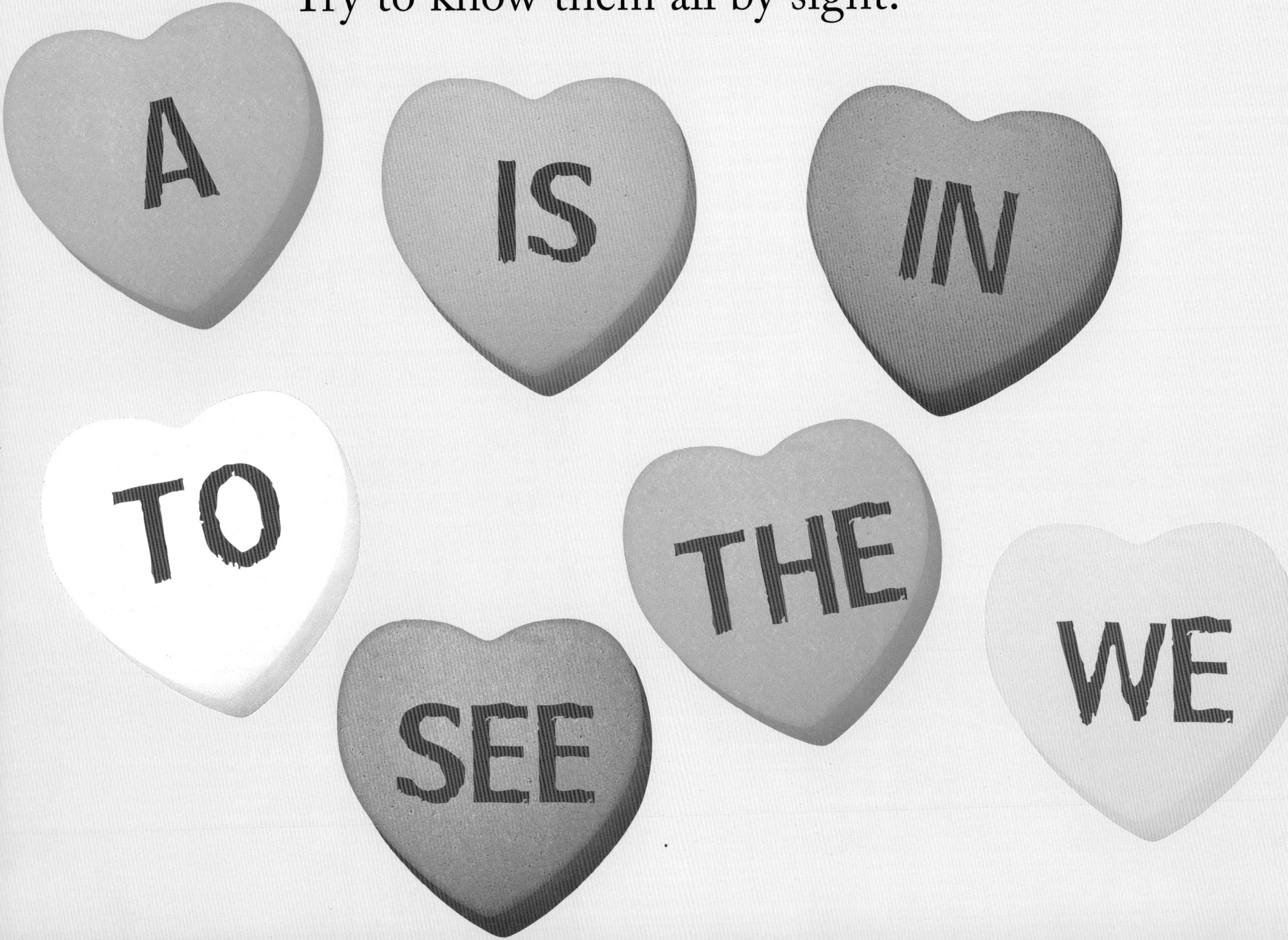

A

IS

IN

TO

SEE

THE

WE

A, is, in, to, see, the, we.
And, I, can, up, go, it, me.

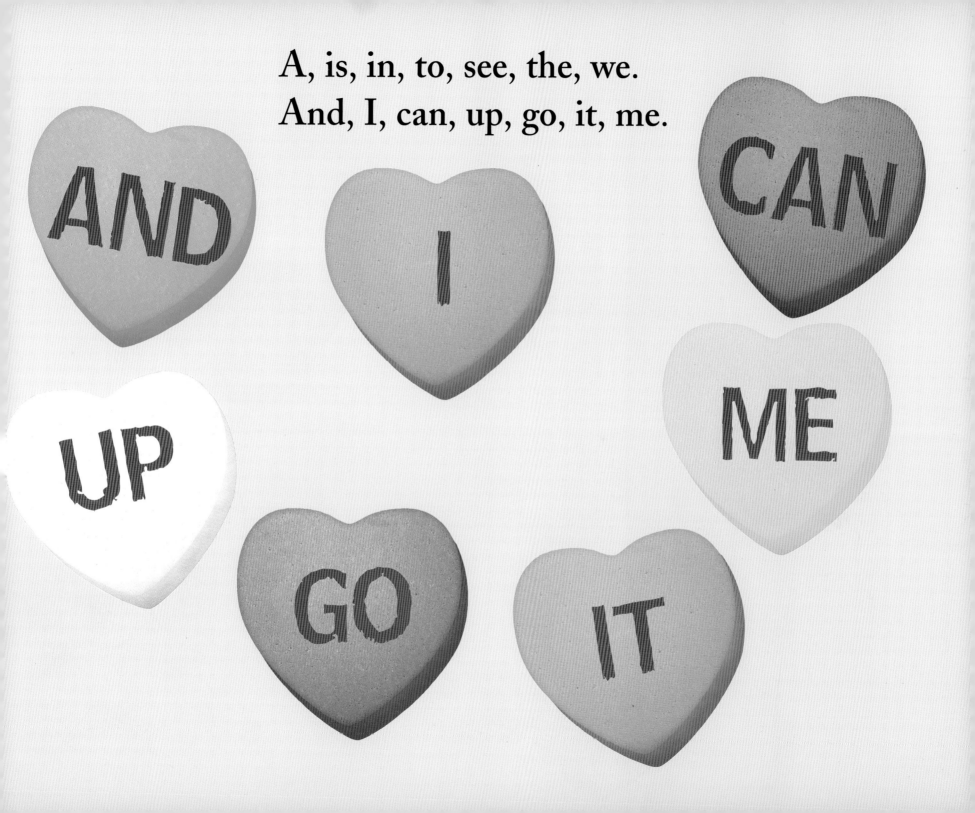

While reading words you will learn to spell—
Met, made, bus, home, this, box, tell.

MET

MADE

BUS

HOME

THIS

BOX

TELL

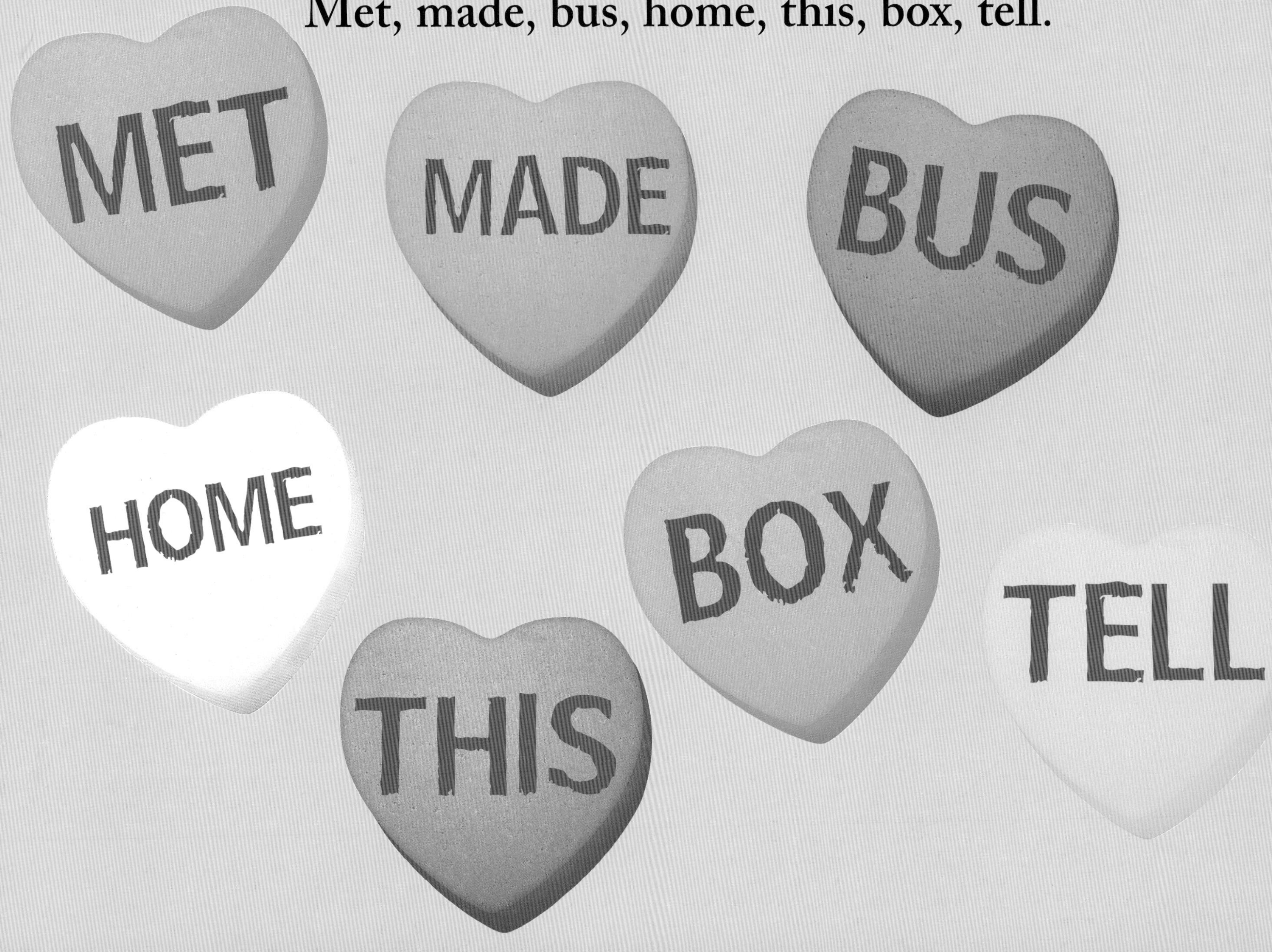

That was fun. Let's try some more—
Day, out, food, think, time, said, for!

Run, red, cat, big, come, like, look.
Here, play, this, on, read a book!

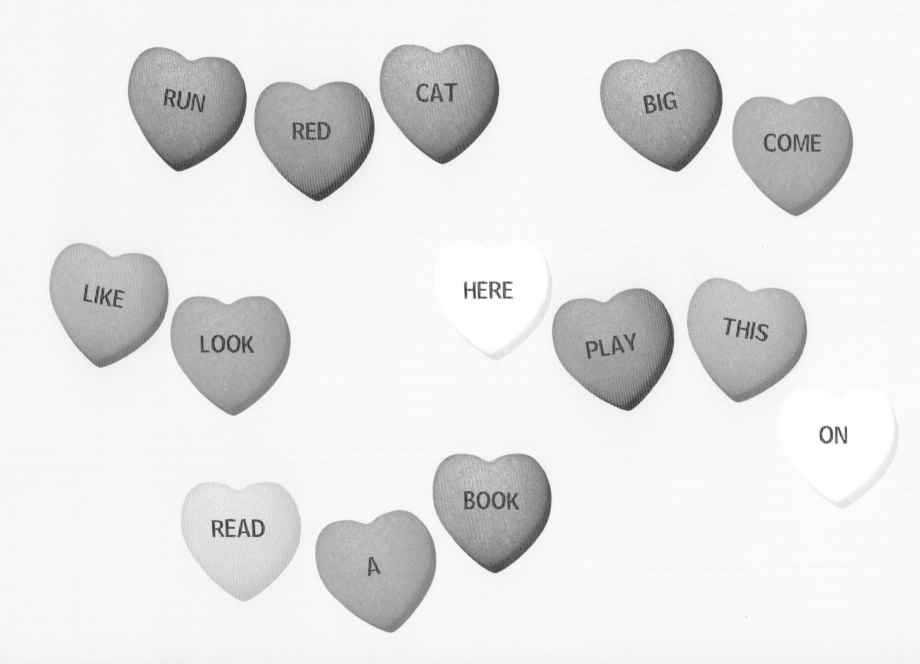

Look closely to read: **the, they, there, that, then.**
Words can answer—**Who? What? Where? Why? When?**

These words are the numbers from **one** to **ten**.
To know them well, read them again.

Purple, orange, green, yellow, pink, and white.
The words mean the color. Did you read them right?

Here are more colors for you to do.
Read each one: **red, black, brown, blue.**

RED   BLACK   BROWN   BLUE

Contractions are two words turned into one.
An apostrophe means the job's been done.
Has not is **hasn't, will not** is **won't.**
Is not is **isn't, do not** is **don't.**

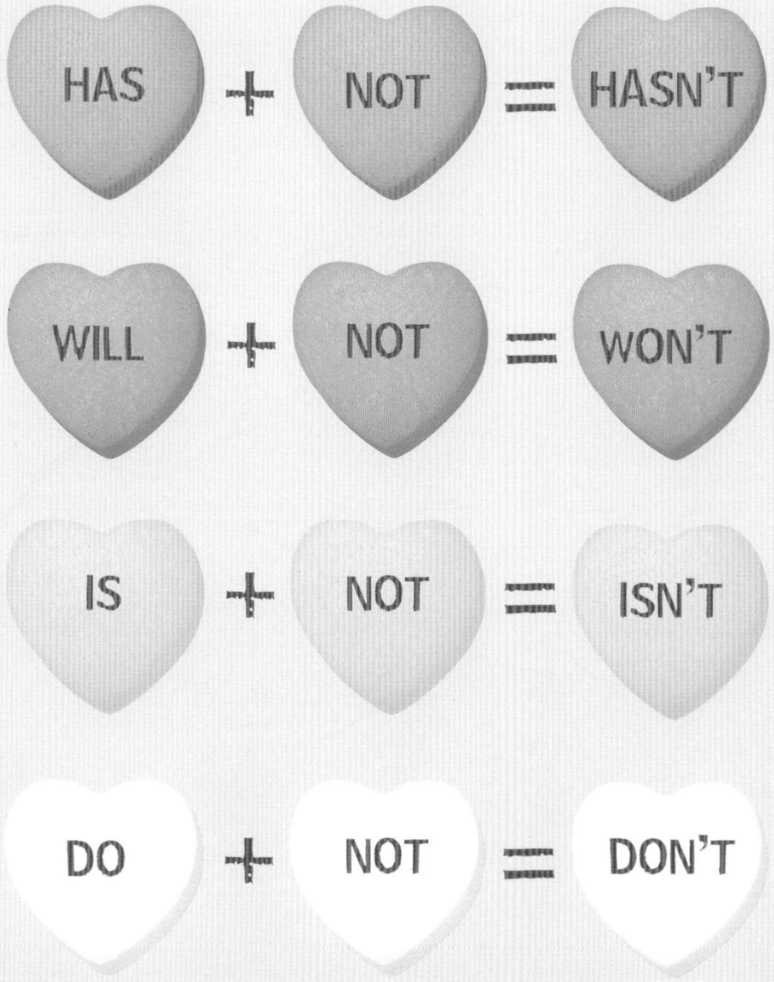

HAS + NOT = HASN'T

WILL + NOT = WON'T

IS + NOT = ISN'T

DO + NOT = DON'T

Compound words can be a lot of fun.
Find two words that make up one.

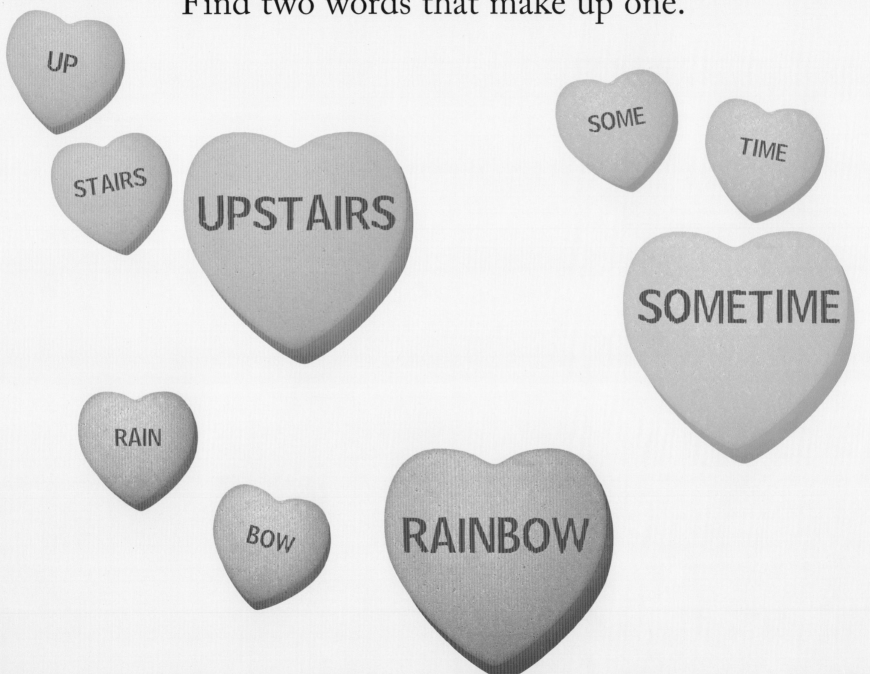

Upstairs, sometime, and **rainbow**,
Bedtime, sunshine. Now you know.

Words that sound alike are said to rhyme.
You can learn to do it in no time.
Make–cake, book–look, see–me–tree.
Jump–bump, big–pig, he–knee–three.

Hop–pop, box–fox, go–no–grow.
Feet–meet, ring–sing, low–tow–show.

Opposite words are far from the same.
Think of some—it's like a game!
On–off, up–down, stop and **go.**
Push–pull, in–out, yes and **no.**

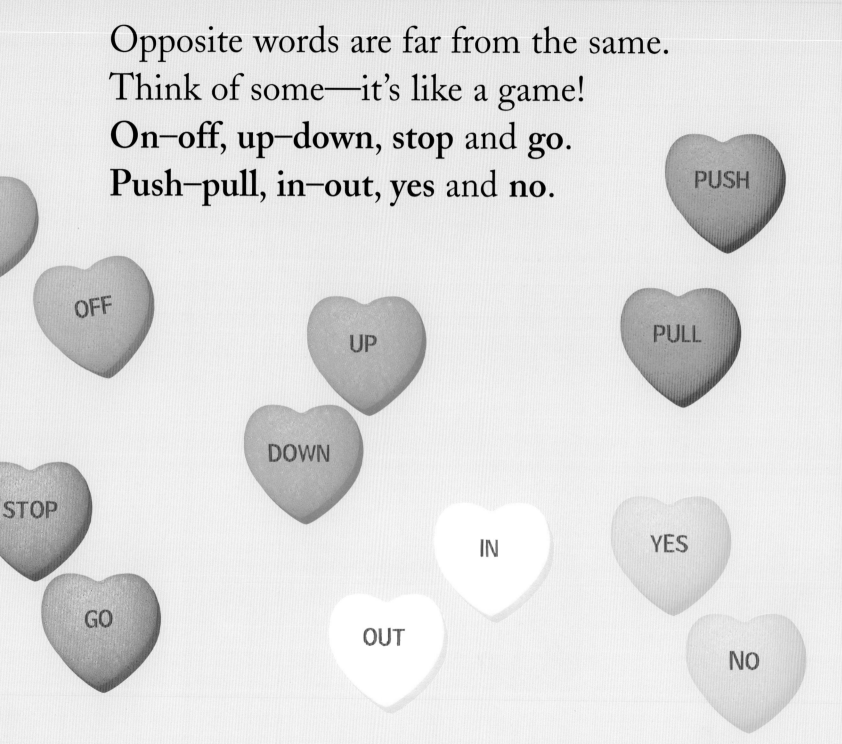

These opposite words might make you grin.
Big–small, **short**–**tall**, **fat** and **thin**.

Dog, cat, bird, sheep, bear, and **snake.**
Words say the sounds that these words make.

Woof, meow, tweet, baa, roar, and **hiss.**
Did you know reading would sound like this?

Words make you feel good for a long while.
Hello, hug, kiss, good, love, and **smile.**

Call me. Be mine. You're my friend ...

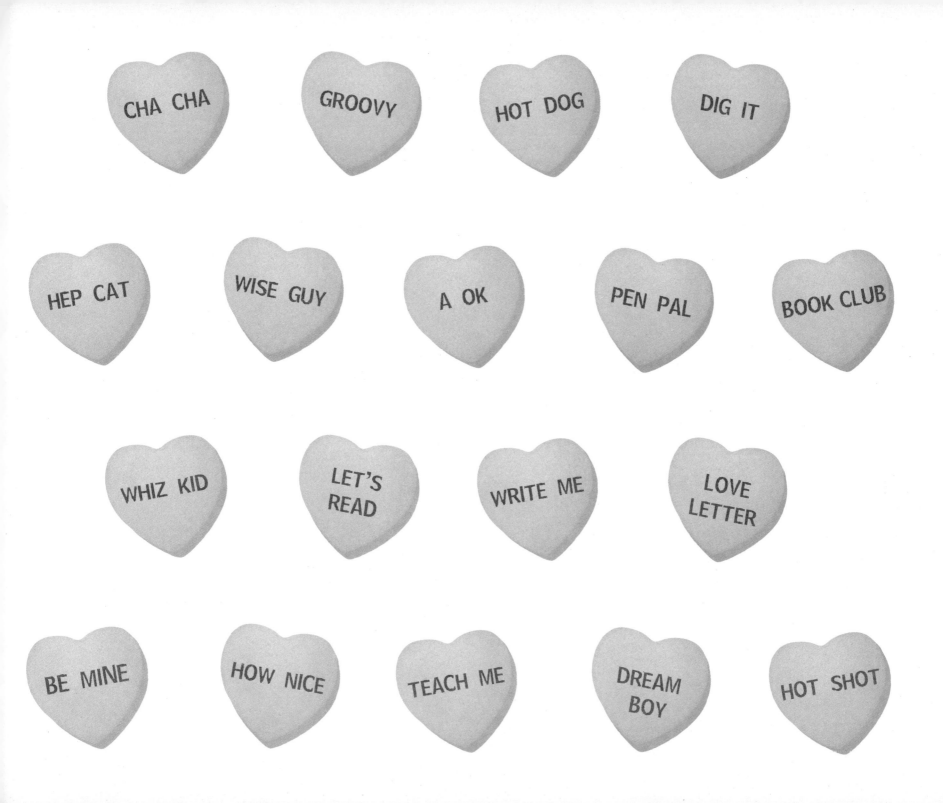

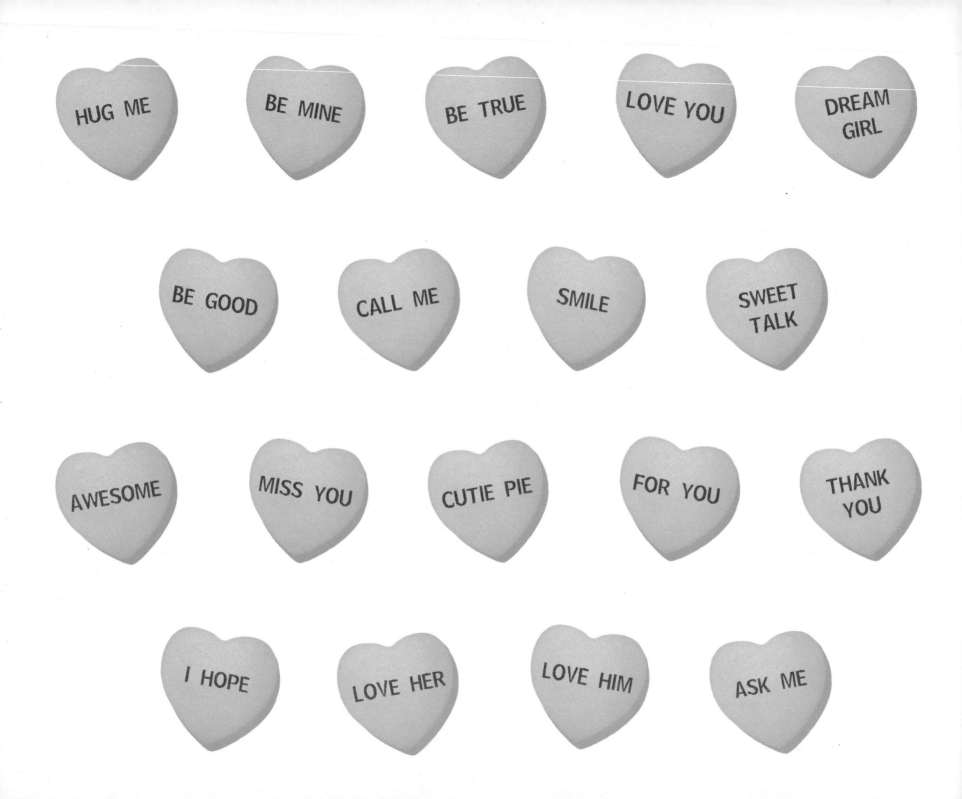